The
Culinary
Adventures
►of a ◄
Brooklyn
Bodega Cat

H.K. Scribnick

ARCHWAY
PUBLISHING

Archway Publishing books may be ordered
through booksellers or by contacting:

Archway Publishing
1663 Liberty Drive
Bloomington, IN 47403
www.archwaypublishing.com
844-669-3957

ISBN: 978-1-6657-5397-5 (sc)
ISBN: 978-1-6657-5398-2 (e)

Library of Congress Control Number: 2023923135

Print information available on the last page.

Archway Publishing rev. date: 12/18/2023

For my parents, Doris and Sanford, who instilled
in me a love of reading and the beauty of fiction to
transport us into the world of our imaginations.

"To write is to prevent forgetting"
Annie Ernaux
2022 Nobel Prize in Literature

"Seven is the number I will always be loving…"

Karameh, Wael. "A Little Story: Number 7 ★★★ ★★★ ★." 2009.
Poem Hunter, www.poemhunter.com

CHAPTER 1

The Origin Story

HE WAS BORN shortly after his sister at 7 a.m. on July 7, 2021, the progeny of some alley cats living beneath "Mr. Coco's Bodega" on the corner of Vanderbilt and Myrtle in the heart of Brooklyn Heights. Their parents had settled in a few days earlier, sensing that their brood would be arriving soon. (You might wonder what a bodega is and I'm here to clear things up: In New York City, where Brooklyn Heights is located, a bodega is a neighborhood convenience store and, in this case, there was also a small counter for breakfast, lunch and snacks.) The cats had created a cool and comfortable environment and hoped no one would discover their hideaway, forcing them to leave before the litter was born.

Actually, Mr. Coco's Bodega was managed by Mr. Woo who had leased the small corner store a few months earlier after receiving official permission to immigrate to New York City. Mr. Woo was thrilled to be in the United States, welcoming the chance to leave the small town of Icheon in South Korea, just outside the capital city of Seoul. His sister Mina also resided in the United States having married an American citizen she met on a college exchange program. Mina described the borough of Brooklyn to Mr. Woo as a vibrant, unique community within the vast, electrifying community of New York City. She believed her brother would quickly integrate into American society by managing the bodega. At the time, Mr. Woo could never have imagined he'd soon be sharing the shop with some additional residents.

Indeed, the bodega turned out to be the ideal place to begin building his new life in the United States. Mr. Woo swiftly ingratiated himself within the neighborhood and the sidewalk in front of the shop became a favorite spot for residents to congregate: from 7 a.m., when Mr. Woo lifted the heavy metal jalousie, to 7 p.m., when he was obliged to close shop because of the past year's pandemic. He had set up seven small tables outside the bodega at which everyone could feel safe and left the front door and big picture window wide open so he could enjoy the noises and smells of the City while busy at work.

On this particular day in July, Mr. Woo had been a bit sluggish coming down from his upstairs apartment to set up the big coffee machine in the bodega. You could almost predict that it would need to be refilled at least seven times by about eleven a.m. But it was only 6:07 a.m. on this glorious summer morning and very quiet when he became aware of what he thought were tiny mews coming from somewhere beneath the thin floorboards at the back of the shop...

It had recently occurred to Mr. Woo that, when emptying the bodega's trash in the dumpsters behind the shop, there had been what appeared to be, a small trail of shredded cheese leading directly into a narrow crack in the foundation. His initial assumption had been that someone from the pizzeria next door was a bit careless with the trash and had perhaps dropped some bits of parmesan along the way. So now, as he placed the "Back in 7 minutes" sign in the front door of the bodega, and made his way into the rear alley towards the bins, he suspected something else might be going on under the floorboards.

Mr. Woo quickly dropped down onto his scrawny knees; he was a slight man of 5'7" weighing just 127 pounds. At first, after putting his ear up to the concrete foundation he didn't detect anything out of the ordinary but a few seconds later the distinct meowing sound of kittens became evident. He got out his flashlight, which he always carried in his front pants pocket just in case of a power outage, and shined it through the opening in the foundation. He was startled to see, looking back at him, seven sets of tiny eyes.

What to do? In his belief that cats were the bearers of good fortune, Mr. Woo had no intention of disturbing this troupe. He made his way back to the bodega, opened a few tins of cat food and returned to the alley. After slowly sliding the food through the opening, he pledged to check on the feline family early the next morning.

The following day was excessively warm, probably due to the fact that New York is such a densely-built brick and mortar city with way too few green spaces. The thermometer outside the bodega was already registering 87 degrees and it was only 11 a.m. Mr. Woo had been quite busy serving up lots of iced coffee and hadn't had a chance to check on the kittens at the back of the shop. When there was finally a break in customers, he put the "Back in 7 minutes" sign on the front door again and hurried into the alley, balancing two bowls of water as he ran. He knelt down, put his ear to the wall and listened. Pretty quiet…. He retrieved his flashlight, directed it into the opening and was surprised to see only two sets of eyes staring back at him. Where were the others? Had these two creatures been left alone? Unable to answer his own questions, and with customers certainly lining up at the bodega door, Mr. Woo carefully slipped the water under the foundation and left.

After closing that evening, Mr. Woo scurried swiftly to the back of the shop with some cat food and illuminated the area under the foundation. Again, only two sets of eyes peering back at him… This does not bode well, he thought, and as he contemplated what the next course of action should be, one set of eyes began to gradually approach the opening in the wall. Mr. Woo stumbled back excitedly as a tiny brown and black paw became visible. And then just as quickly disappeared as he reached out to touch it. Having never had cats of his own, he decided it would be wise to speak with Mike and Pam for advice, regulars at the bodega who only ever effused about the virtues of their own two whiskered friends.

   The next morning Mike and Pam came into the shop and requested "the usual" combo platter for breakfast. Luckily no one else was waiting in line behind them. Mr. Woo was very fond of the couple since they had helped fill out much of the paperwork required for him to stay in New York. Mike was a beefy fellow with tattooed arms, so many tattoos in fact that there was no room left for any more. He was extremely proud of the colorful designs running up and down his muscular arms and only ever wore short-sleeved T-shirts, even in the middle of winter. Pam, on the other hand, was a petite, thin woman and almost always appeared in button-down gingham shirts worn together with black pencil skirts and tights coordinated to match her tops. An unlikely couple but so in love.

   After learning of the kittens Mr. Woo had discovered, Mike and Pam were quick to offer their assistance. The three traipsed back into the alley behind the bodega. As soon as Mr. Woo shined his light under the foundation, four tiny paws cautiously appeared. First the brown and black paws and then hesitatingly, two tiny and very dainty gray ones. It was clear to Mike and Pam that the kittens had been abandoned and explained to Mr. Woo that drastic measures were necessary. The couple offered to bring the kittens to an animal shelter located just a few blocks from the bodega. This seemed especially prudent as, coming around the corner this very moment was Chief, the black, extremely large and ferocious German Shepherd dog who stood guard over the neighboring pizzeria. However sad, the kittens had obviously been left to fend for themselves.

Rosie had been living in Manhattan with her father Doug for about seven months. She and her dad worked quite contentedly in the City but always felt that something was missing when they arrived home at the end of the day. It became clear to Rosie that an intervention was necessary knowing that both of them were accustomed to living in homes filled with pets.

Together with her friend Courtney, Rosie decided to take an outing the following Saturday to Hudson River Park on 14th Street, one of several sites throughout the City participating in a citywide animal adoption event. Her hope was to surprise Doug with a warm, furry creature if she was fortunate enough to sense some chemistry with one of the four-legged adoptees.

The girls arrived at the park mid-morning and were surprised to see hundreds of people roaming about admiring a wide assortment of animals waiting patiently, or not, to connect with a human caregiver. Rosie and Courtney were particularly struck by the number of dogs with signs "Adopt Me" strung around their necks. Knowing she and Doug wouldn't be able to provide the care and attention one of these frisky hounds deserved, Rosie strolled over to an area which appeared to be the hub for cat adoptions.

She and Courtney soon struck up a conversation with one of the many non-profit organizations which had brought rescue cats to the event. Their representative, Iris, had only two teeny kittens still available but Rosie was hesitant that they were just too young. In response, Iris suggested Rosie check out two older kittens she had in her truck which was parked just a few feet away, explaining that these cats were a "bonded pair", i.e. siblings, in this case brother and sister. But she also made clear her promise to the animal shelter, which had received the kittens from a large tattooed man and his girlfriend: they would only be adopted together.

Seventeen months later......

The kittens, discovered at the back of a truck and brought home as a surprise for Rosie's father, soon responded to their new monikers: Otto and Gidget. The two fabulous felines often found themselves home alone after Rosie and Doug went off to work and knew this was an opportunity to be as good or bad as they pleased. Nap time was always first on the agenda. Cuddled together like yin and yang on the soft, cozy velvet couch, they would get a little shut eye for a few minutes after which Otto would stretch out his paws, get up on all fours, circle around his sister and begin to clean behind her ears. Gidget had difficulty reaching there and relied upon her brother to keep her squeaky clean. She would stir affectionately, lift her chin and hope Otto would get under there as well. In return, she would groom Otto's neck...Next, the two would slip off the couch and move into the sun-filled corner near the bookcase where nap time resumed.

Otto had grown tremendously over the past year and when he stretched his slender body out entirely, he was probably more than two feet long. The brown and black silky stripes arching over his back hid the most wonderful, honey-colored stomach and now, lying on his side snoozing in the sun, it would have been a real treat for anyone lucky enough to be nearby.

At first glance, Gidget appeared to have solid-colored, fluffy, pale gray fur but upon closer inspection, she was actually striped as well. And that tummy, a sumptuous ivory color, almost grazed the floor when she walked: Gidget loved cat food but didn't like to move around that much. Thus, the largish tummy.... Otto, on the other hand, also loved cat food but was especially fond of people food.

After adopting Otto and Gidget, Rosie could sense that her life would change dramatically because of their presence. At mealtime it became evident that Otto was not just a dry, cat-food-kind of cat, but had very discriminating taste. Gidget observed in amazement as her brother spent dinnertime on Rosie's lap constantly trying to sample everything she ate. It was sometimes rather annoying but it was clear to Rosie that Otto was indeed quite unique. His favorite food was cheese but not just any sort of cheese. For some strange reason he had a preference for parmesan. I'm sure you recall a trail of shredded cheese leading under a bodega foundation. Well, Otto did too.

It now gives me great pleasure to report that Otto and Gidget have accompanied Rosie on some amazing culinary adventures, chronicled in the pages which follow. You will come to know these feline siblings in so many ways: savvy travelers, discriminating foodies, and keen observers of cultures so different to ours in the United States. They have "relish"-ed every opportunity to test the waters for new experiences and especially, and that goes predominantly for Otto, to try new food.

CHAPTER 2

Otto Goes Deep: Cheese Fondue (Verbier, Switzerland)

ROSIE AND AXEL had been living together for two years and seven months when they decided to take their first overseas trip to Verbier, located in the heart of the Swiss Alps. Axel had first learned to ski in Verbier at the age of three and now wanted to share those experiences with his girl, Rosie. The two had met almost four years earlier but hadn't realized at the time they were destined to spend their futures together. It just took a bit longer than either could have known. But after Rosie left New York City they reconnected and the rest, they say, was **cat**hartic.

Where Rosie and Axel traveled so did Otto and Gidget; they never went anywhere without the two cats. This being Otto and Gidget's first airplane trip, Axel and Rosie were pretty anxious on how events might transpire. The flight from Washington D.C., where they now lived, to Geneva, Switzerland, was sure to be a challenge. After consulting their vet, Dr. Jean prescribed some knock-out sleeping pills. She had tried the pills on her own Maine Coon cat and this twenty-seven pound, lumbering kitty was lights-out within seventeen minutes.

Two days before the trip, Rosie thought it would be a good idea to try out the sleeping pills on Otto and Gidget so she and Axel would know what to expect. Of course, Gidget didn't even realize that she had ingested the pill which Rosie tucked into her cat food since she was feeling particularly snacky that day. Gobbled it right up. Within a few minutes Gidget began to gingerly teeter around the apartment. She dropped to her side and then sprawled onto her back, legs bent, knees facing up toward the ceiling. But Otto was a different story.

Rosie tried to sneak the sleepy-making pill into his dry food but he was having none of that. After the first bite, he gagged and - voilà! - out popped the pill. Rosie tried hiding the pill in some tuna - Otto loved tuna. But again, no luck - out came the pill. And then, what do you think she did? Yes. She went to the fridge and cut a small chunk of …… parmesan cheese. She slipped the pill into the cheese, dangled it in front of Otto who in turn, quickly gulped it down. Soon his lean, lanky frame became even leaner and lankier as he succumbed to the effects of the pill and he abruptly splayed out on the floor, paws extended forward and back - it seemed as if he had grown an additional seven inches.

Otto and Gidget were now both in what you might call a **cat**atonic state. It was almost as if they had lost all the bones in their bodies: walking became difficult and so they resorted to various splayed-out positions. This was about all they were capable of. What a relief. Perhaps the trip across the Atlantic would not be as stressful as Rosie and Axel had imagined…..

On the morning of their departure to Switzerland, Rosie and Axel finished packing up and the apartment was in purrfect order. The final step was to coax the cats into their "transportation housing units"…Gidget and Otto would need to stay in a mesh carry-on case, about seventeen inches long, for the duration of the flight. The cases would be slipped under the seats in front of Rosie and Axel…. not particularly comfortable but this was required by the airline.

Prior to the journey, Rosie had prepped the cats so they might accustom themselves to being confined to these containers. She placed the cases on the dining room table with **cat**nip and bits of cheese inside. The zippers on the top and sides of the housing units were left open for Otto and Gidget to come and go as they pleased. The cats adapted to them pretty easily and were soon pawing playfully at each other over the tops, **cat**napping during the day, and using them to stand guard over the apartment like a pair of sphinxes while Rosie and Axel went about their business.

In the end the cats, as well as Rosie and Axel, survived the plane trip to Geneva fairly well. The first hour had been a bit stressful as Otto and Gidget **cat**called to one another and meowed at a decibel level even the plane's engines were unable to mask. Initially, the passengers seated around them smiled politely but you could tell they had all been tempted to jump up and ask the flight attendants if they could change their seats. Eventually the cats did settle down and following a relatively quiet seven hour and fifty-seven minute flight the plane landed in Geneva, Switzerland.

Axel and Rosie were now seated in their rental car and about to leave Geneva airport for the drive to Verbier. They were finally able to release Otto and Gidget from their transportation housing units so they could roam freely about the car. In addition, the rental company had ensured that a litter box would be in the vehicle upon their arrival so the cats could take care of all their kitty needs.

As soon as Axel had unzipped the top and sides of the units, Otto slithered out hesitatingly to explore these yet again new surroundings. Gidget was not quite ready. Otto teetered around the rear of the car and then, with front paws stretched out, slid over the top of the second row back seat as if he were a giant puddle. It would obviously take more time until he had regained control of any muscles. He did succeed, however, in making it to the front passenger seat and passed out almost immediately as he snuggled into Rosie's lap. A few minutes later Gidget powered through her daze, stumbled up to the front seat, slid behind Otto, and the two slept the rest of the way to Verbier.

Rosie and Axel were quickly ensconced in their condominium rental and couldn't wait to hit the ski slopes for a week of fun. Otto and Gidget were content to bask in the sun and didn't mind at all when they had the place to themselves. However, an important reason for Axel wanting to share this overseas adventure with Rosie was a special restaurant his parents had taken him to many years ago. Not only was the restaurant known for typical "Valais" cuisine (Valais is one of 26 cantons, or states, in Switzerland and situated in the southwestern part of the country) but it was also the only restaurant in the area to welcome pets.

The owners of this unique restaurant, "Chez Fromage", more on that to come, had a pair of Bernese Mountain dogs who were also quite welcoming to animal guests showing up with humans in tow. These two big beautiful pups, also a bonded pair (sisters), assisted in coordinating treats for whatever assortment of creatures happen to show up: cockatoos, ferrets, turtles, geckos, or the usual cats and dogs. When the restaurant was filled on any given occasion, it was a lively **cat**ophony (oops cacophony...typo), rife with yips, yaps, mews, shrieks and squawks emanating from under or over the tables. Indeed, there were only seven tables and this kept things somewhat in check, but you never knew how the evening would pan out.

Otto and Gidget could sense something unusual was about

to happen when they were placed in their transportation housing for the trip to "Chez Fromage". Axel and Rosie would not be driving their rental car to the restaurant. Instead, there was a gondola operating from the center of Verbier which traveled down to mid-mountain where the restaurant was located. For those of you who have never been in a gondola before, imagine you are sitting in an enclosed cabin, suspended high in the air, and moving across terrain you would not normally be able to cross very easily. I mean cliffs, gorges, or even water. Gondolas are not particularly suited for those suffering from acrophobia. This gondola was also not like the floating kind which we will experience in our next chapter.

The gondola trip was all part of the excitement for the evening and only those with reservations at "Chez Fromage", for themselves and their pets, were allowed to use it. The cats had to stay confined until they were safely inside the restaurant since the gondola had been designed without any glass in the window frames and no one wanted to take a chance that Otto and Gidget would find that overly interesting.

As the foursome glided quietly through the brilliant night sky sheltered within their gondola, they caught glimpses back to the twinkling town of Verbier. It almost appeared that at any moment the town could slip into the abyss below since it had been built right up to the edge of a great cliff. In addition to the many homes or "chalets", as they are called here, and quaint Swiss hotels, Rosie and Axel could even see their apartment from the lift. The evening sky was dazzling: stars crystal clear and illuminating the snow-covered mountains which now seemed to surround them as the gondola descended peacefully down the slope.

So, let's get back to this appropriately-named restaurant, "Chez Fromage". Verbier is located in the French-speaking portion of Switzerland. (There are also three other languages spoken in this small country: German, Italian and Romansh.) Dig deep into a French/English dictionary or just take a wild guess: what do you think "Fromage" means? And why do you think Axel wanted to take everyone, especially Otto, to this cozy, super charming locale on the edge of a steep mountain cliff? Think hard. How about CHEESE? Yes, the specialty of "Chez Fromage", or literally "home of cheese", was cheese fondue. And who better to delight in this altogether delectable, alpine treat than Otto?

Such excitement. At the door of "Chez Fromage", everyone was greeted by Eveala and Clochette, the Bernese mountain dog sisters. The "girls" were wearing traditional cow bells around their necks held in place by elaborately embroidered bands decorated with miniature people wearing traditional alpine costumes: Trachtens, Lederhosen and Dirndls (i.e., decorative jackets, leather pants and poofy dresses). More importantly, these bells came in handy for Eveala and Clochette's owners since the two dogs loved to disappear into the hills surrounding the restaurant to sniff out marmots which lived in small caves. The bells allowed them to always be heard.

The sisters were especially wound up this evening since the restaurant was fully booked. Reservations had been placed by humans bringing an unusual assortment of animals: a bearded vulture chick and an ibex, among others, ….and, of course, Otto and Gidget.

Upon arrival, Rosie and Axel were led to one of the seven

tables which had been set with traditional red and white gingham tablecloths, dishes decorated with alpine scenes and the requisite fondue forks. (These secure cubes of baguette bread as they are dipped into a piping hot pot of melted cheese.) Otto and Gidget had the option of either sitting on puffy, forest-green, velvet pillows, mouths at table height or, since the rules of etiquette were suspended at "Chez Fromage", disavowing of course what everyone has been taught as a child, paws and/or elbows were allowed on the table. Either way, the cats had clear access to their plates.

When the fondue arrived, Axel tied a green cloth napkin around Otto's neck; Gidget would have none of that but did seem curious about the boiling pot of cheese now situated at the center of the table. The aroma was magnificent. Otto was ready.

Axel dunked a piece of bread into the pot, twirled it around in the cheese, pulled it out to cool a bit and then....Otto had his first taste. Total bliss, awe inspiring. The fusion of three local cheeses, appenzellar, gruyere and vacherin, came together with such amazing impact that Otto could hardly control himself as he waited for the next bite. Now sitting, or shall we say standing on Rosie's lap, front paws on the red and white checked tablecloth, he wriggled with delight until he could savor the next bite. As each piece of bread was dunked into the hot cheese mixture, his ears would wiggle. Even Gidget tried a nibble but decided that she much preferred lounging on the red velvet chair next to the fireplace. The waiter offered everyone a sip of Kirschwasser, a cherry liqueur, which supposedly helps with digestion but really just tastes divine mid-fondue (to adult humans, of course). Otto and Gidget didn't seem very interested in sampling the clear liquid after poking their noses into the small etched glasses. But when Rosie and Axel sipped their samples of Kirschwasser, a smooth, warm sensation slid down their throats.

The evening was a complete success. All pets and human guests lined up on their way out of "Chez Fromage" to personally thank the owners for a spectacular meal and the traditional Swiss experience. Eveala and Clochette barked their goodbyes and, once all the guests had departed, headed toward their doggy beds which were tucked away under the wooden rafters at the back of the restaurant for a well-deserved sleep.

Rosie and Axel strolled towards the gondola for the return trip up the mountain to Verbier. They had placed Otto and Gidget, now drowsy from all the warm cheese they had consumed, back into their transportation housing. They smiled at each other and thought this had certainly been one of the best meals they had ever shared and such a unique opportunity to indulge in Otto's favorite food: cheese.

Traditional Cheese Fondue

2 pounds shredded Appenzellar
1 pound shredded Gruyère
Optional: 1/8 pound Vacherin
2 garlic cloves
Nutmeg
Ground pepper
Kirschwasser (grown up beverage)
Corn starch
Dry white wine (grown up beverage)
Baguette

Serves 4-6

Rub an earthenware fondue pot with both sides of a split garlic clove. Mince another clove of garlic and place in the pot. On the stovetop, add a handful of the mixed cheeses as well as a splash of wine and warm on medium heat until the cheese begins to melt, stirring constantly. Increase heat slightly and continue to add handfuls of cheese and splashes of wine until the mixture is fluid and smooth. Remember to keep stirring so the cheese does not stick to the bottom of the pot. Once all the cheese is melted, add a mixture of about 2 tablespoons cornstarch, 1 tablespoon kirschwasser, dash of nutmeg and ground pepper and stir until slightly thickened. Taste test for more spices or thicken with more corn starch, if needed. Remove pot from stove and place on a rechaud (small burner) which has been set on a dining table and is set to low heat. Eat immediately by dunking ¼-inch-sized cubes of crunchy baguette using fondue forks. After immersing the bread in the hot cheese, pull out the fork and rest it on the edge of the pot. Twirl the cheese until it stops dripping and is cool enough to pop into your mouth.

CHAPTER 3

Otto Plunges Into Pizza
(Venice, Italy)

ROSIE AND AXEL were celebrating their seventh anniversary and had decided to visit one of the most famous cities in the world, Venice, Italy. They had practiced their Italian diligently well in advance of the trip and brushed up on the country's customs to prepare for the usual encounters or mishaps one experiences when traveling. Had Otto and Gidget realized the potential fishing opportunities Venice's shallow lagoon could offer, they would have been doing some serious prep work as well.

And where there is water there are fish: sardines, eels, anchovies and shellfish like mussels, clams and scallops. Gidget was particularly gifted with a delicate "scoop and lift" technique she had honed at home while eating from the apportioned dish Axel insisted upon which limited the cats' ability to snorf up all their food at once. Gidget's talent might "serve" her well in Venice.

If you don't know much about Venice then prepare for the trip of a lifetime. The city is not only overly enchanting but especially unique in that you can only get there by boat. In addition, it is of major relevance since it is considered a "World Heritage Site". This means that the city is legally protected by an international convention due to its significance and outstanding value to humanity. This convention is administered by the United Nations Educational, Scientific and Cultural Organization (UNESCO). So get ready. Venice is an architectural masterpiece unlike anywhere else in the world.

After leaving Milan International Airport into which they had flown, Rosie and Axel steered their rental car eastward toward the very top of Italy's "boot" where Venice is located. (Check this out on a map and you'll see why Italy is referred to as such.) Since no cars are allowed within the city, all of Rosie and Axel's belongings would be transferred from their vehicle to a boat and then from the boat to their hotel, so they had packed very lightly. In addition to the required carry-on cases for Otto and Gidget, they had brought only two overly-stuffed backpacks. Axel had reserved a parking spot in advance at a garage on the mainland of Italy in the city of Tronchetteo. From there they would take a motor boat to their hotel. After that, the vast majority of their excursions would be on Venice's renowned gondolas.

Otto and Gidget had never been on a boat before and even though they were still a bit punchy from the airplane, they were nonetheless very curious about the swaying and jolting going on all around them. Wafts of sea water had their noses tingling and they were curiously aware that something was afloat. They were. Noses pressed up against the mesh of their carrying cases, hoping for them to be unzipped.

The motor boat slowly pulled away from the dock at Tronchetteo and soon entered a narrow canal bordered on both sides by mostly seven-storied, multi-colored, stone facades. After traveling through the waterway for a few minutes, the captain pulled up to an open, massive wooden door over which a red and gold fabric banner flapped gently in the breeze. The flag was resplendent with an image of a noble-looking lady, maybe a duchess, a countess? Axel and Rosie looked at each other and wondered why the boat had landed here. What now? Their concern was soon assuaged as they observed the captain lifting a ladder off the side of the boat and handing it up to a gentleman dressed in uniform; the same image depicted on the banner above the door also adorned the left breast pocket of the man's jacket. This must be the hotel. How strange to walk, hmmm climb, up a ladder and into a hotel. With backpacks and cats, the group stepped cautiously into the "Palazzo" Abadessa. That sounds pretty noble, too.

How shall I describe these Venetian accommodations? A step back in time? Stuck in time? Regardless, the "Palazzo" Abadessa was jaw-droppingly refined, regal. The group traipsed behind the bellhop through what appeared to be an elegant ballroom, tapestries adorning every wall, huge oriental carpets covering the creaking wood floors, and ceilings at least twentyseven feet high. Arriving at the reception desk which was tucked beneath a spiral stone staircase, they were greeted by a young woman who welcomed them to the "Palazzo". (Now that I have used this word several times you might be wondering what it means. If you think it sounds a lot like "Palace" you are correct.) Yes, Palazzo Abadessa was an historical palace built in the year 1540. That's almost 500 years old.

After checking in and receiving a brief orientation of the city, Axel and Rosie were escorted to their room by the concierge, or porter, by way of the grand staircase. They could almost envision how the Palazzo's original occupants might have wowed their guests as they descended these ornate steps, dressed in all their finery. The concierge led the group to a very large yet exceedingly charming guest room which was decorated with antique furniture, silks and massive historical paintings. He wished them a pleasant stay by pronouncing, as he exited quietly: "Spero che si trovi bene qui!" And how could it not be in such magnificent surroundings? Rosie and Axel looked at each other and smiled simultaneously as they saw Gidget and Otto snuggled up together on the elegant canopied bed.

But the gang was hungry. They had missed both dinner and breakfast on their flight over the Atlantic Ocean. Axel was now sitting in the private, enclosed garden of the Palazzo as Otto and Gidget were free to explore: there was no way to escape. Don't think they didn't try but they seemed more intrigued by the great marble sculptures, lush plantings and tall, narrow cypress trees adorning the courtyard. Of particular interest was a large antique pushcart piled high with colorful flowers. Gidget had already disappeared amongst the blooms and Otto was perplexed as to where his sister might be.

Rosie was in the hotel foyer standing beneath a low-timbered ceiling as she interviewed the concierge for suggestions on where to find some traditional Venetian cuisine together with the cats. Her idea was to combine an early dinner with a visit to one of the most famous islands of Venice: Murano.

Murano is such a popular destination that the concierge recommended calling ahead to "Ristorante Marlin" to ensure that a table would be available. The restaurant was situated adjacent to the Rio dei Vetrai, one of the major canals running through Murano and yes, the concierge was told, they could accommodate the group. Reservation complete but now how to get there?

The surprise was organized by Rosie and after corralling the cats and Axel, who was napping contentedly under a eucalyptus tree, she led them all back to the door through which they had entered the hotel. Waiting below the doorway was a long, narrow, banana-shaped, flat-bottomed boat with a tall front stem and even taller back stern. This was to be their first gondola ride through the narrow waterways of Venice.

Gondolas are quite ornate and many of the carved shapes and figures adorning these boats are symbolic of famous locations in this city of islands: the twists and turns sculpted into the sides of a gondola depict the Canal Grande, the main waterway through Venice; a comb-like shape represents the six districts of the city; a curved form at the top of a gondola is reminiscent of the headwear worn by a Doge, the noble head-of-state during medieval times. And depictions of the main islands of Venice, like Murano, Burano and Torcello, might also be part of the gondola's ornamentation.

Standing at the stern was a man sporting a blue- and white-striped top, black pants, a red neckerchief, and a wide-brimmed straw hat: the gondolier. He was holding a long wooden pole and humming what sounded like an Italian folk song.

The gondolier proceeded to help everyone down the ladder and onto the red-padded cushions lining the sides and center bench of the boat. Otto and Gidget had to remain in their traveling cases, as you might assume, but had the bench all to themselves. Rosie and Axel could snuggle at the rear and take in the sights of this incredible city. Romance was in the air. Especially once the gondolier launched the craft away from the Palazzo's pier and began to sing. What a thrilling experience to float peacefully through water, watching ancient buildings slip by as the beautiful tenor voice of the gondolier echoed through the canal: 'O sole mio!

In order to travel through the deeper waters en route to Murano, it was necessary to switch from the gondola to a ferry boat which would drop them off at the southernmost point of the island and quite close to their restaurant. After disembarking at the boat terminal they strolled through passageways of fairytale facades, houses painted in popping hot colors of psychedelic orange, blue, yellow and pink, a feast for the eyes. Not only is Murano known for these crazy colors, it is even more notable for its long history of glass-making factories and galleries. Lining the canals are dozens of places to observe and learn how glassware is produced and to purchase brightly colored glass vases, sculptures and artwork. But let's first get these hungry souls to dinner.

The owners of "Ristorante Marlin" were passionate cat lovers and had created unique seating arrangements for clients wishing to dine with their feline friends. Try to imagine a circular gazebo, almost like an igloo, fully enclosed by screens on seven sides and within, a table surrounded with enough high chairs for visiting cats. And a few seats for human guests as well. Cats "ruled" at this place and the elevated chairs were softly padded for extreme comfort and, like high chairs for babies, had trays on which food could be placed, making it easily accessible to front paws.

The waitstaff at "Ristorante Merlin" had been expecting the group and, upon arrival, they were escorted to a gazebo immediately adjacent to the Rio dei Vetrai canal, giving them a perfect people watching spot. As soon as Rosie and Axel entered, they were able to set Otto and Gidget free since they were now safely confined. After a thorough inspection of their new surroundings, and having caught the aromatic smells emanating from the restaurant's kitchen, the cats sensed another culinary experience "straordinario": extraordinary.

Everyone was famished and the waiter knew time was of the essence. In order to savor Venice's lagoon delicacies he suggested the specialty-of-the-house pizza: seven cheese with, get ready, sardines, eel and other types of seafood. You may know the expression "When in Rome do as the Romans do" but even though this was Venice, they decided to do just that and follow the server's advice.

As Axel and Rosie waited for the pizzas, they reviewed

their plans for the upcoming days in Venice.There were so many sites to see and only limited time to accomplish that. First on the list would be the city's spectacular main plaza, or square, the Piazza San Marco. Here they would visit the Palace of Venice's former rulers, the Doges, who had important ceremonial as well as international responsibilities. The Piazza San Marco has always been the city's focal point and is lined with restaurants and cafes on three sides. But hundreds of years ago the plaza was even more critical for its open air markets at which vendors would sell all sorts of household goods or fresh produce piled high on tables and stalls, supplying the daily necessities to the inhabitants of this remote city. The fourth side of the square opens out onto the city's main thoroughfare, the glorious Grand Canale, and the docks here are the main hub for gondolas and other boats which serve both tourists and locals seeking transportation through and from the city.

Next on the sightseeing list was the Bridge of Sighs and you may wonder where this name came from: the Bridge connects the Doge's Palace to the Old Prison and, in the past, it was quite convenient to send convicts who had just been sentenced in the Palace courtroom immediately to jail or worse, to their execution. Whoa. It was thought that the prisoners "sighed" as they were led over the Bridge to their fate.

Last but not least they would visit the Rialto Bridge, another must-see attraction. The "Ponte di Rialto" remains the world's busiest, suspended marketplace to this day. Shop 'til you drop. Of course all of Axel and Rosie's plans centered around, you guessed it, food. And only those locales which accommodated our furry friends came into consideration.

The pizzas finally arrived and Otto and Gidget could hardly **cat**ain, I mean contain, themselves. Up on hind legs and elevated by their high stools, they waited in ready position as the waiter placed small pre-cut pieces of fishy pizza on their trays. The blend of cheeses was incredible but the addition of fresh, locally-caught fish created a simply delectable pizza: a delicious, delightful, decadent array of the most wonderful seafood they had ever eaten. Until now. Gidget decided that "people" food could actually be quite scrumptious. Even Rosie and Axel, who were not big fans of sardines (who really is?), gobbled up these thin, glistening strips of fish topping their pizzas. They had only ever previously eaten sardines from a can. Living at the source certainly makes a difference. Even the eel was yummy and that's saying a lot when you think about what an eel looks like.

Everyone was filled to the gills (get it?), but there was no way they could pass up dessert. And that dessert would be one of the most famous and popular in Venice i.e., tiramisu. How to describe this fluffy concoction, delicious and with the ability to **cat**apult your taste buds into outer space. In Italian, tiramisu literally means "cheer me up" and it does just that. Constructed of cakey, finger-shaped ladyfingers (sweet biscuits) which have been dipped in coffee and then alternately layered with sweet, creamy mascarpone (soft Italian cream cheese, do you see where this is going?) and then sprinkled with cocoa, tiramisu will knock your socks off. Parmesan cheese is one thing but this mascarpone-filled treat is another. After they were done eating, Otto proceeded to lick everyone's plate cleaner than a dishwasher could ever do. And what a way to end their first meal in the supurrb city of Venice.

Over the next few days, Rosie and Axel took in all the

hotspots, hopping island to island, not even making a dent in visiting the 117-ish islands within Venice's lagoon. They passed through quaint public squares tucked along canals and visited churches where visions and miracles were thought to have occurred. They crossed over many of the 400 plus bridges spanning the Venetian waterways and were already making plans to return before they had even departed, maybe for Carnival? That is one crazy time in February when Venetians party in the streets of the city, dressed in flashy costumes and wearing elaborately painted masks which are often decorated with feathers and gems. Carnival parades and music are categorically wild. Stay tuned.

Homemade Pizza

Pizza crust, either store bought or homemade
Tomato Sauce
Shredded mozzarella cheese
Shredded parmesan cheese
Veggies you love: mushrooms, peppers, tomatoes, onions, any green vegetable, etc. etc.
Fresh basil
Olive oil
Garlic powder

Preheat oven to 475 degrees. Making pizza at home is really a likes vs. dislikes kind of affair. Start by greasing a cookie sheet and then spreading pizza dough to cover it, bringing it up the sides as you prod it with your fingers. Bake the crust alone for about 7 minutes until it starts to brown just a bit. Remove from the oven and spread however much or little (or no!) tomato sauce you like all over the dough and then have fun by adding the veggies and herbs you enjoy. And don't forget the sardines! Or tuna, perhaps? Top it all with handfuls of mozzarella and parmesan, also as much as you like, and drizzle the entire creation with some olive oil. If you love garlic, brush the crust with olive oil and sprinkle it with garlic powder. Bake for about 11 minutes until golden brown and bubbling.

CHAPTER 4

Otto Polishes Off Peruvian Potatoes (Machu Picchu, Peru)

YOU ALL KNOW how much Otto loves cheese. And fish. And meat, which I haven't told you about yet but will when the gang enjoys a unique Russian treat in Colorado. But another one of Otto's favorite foods is the humble potato. Boiled, whipped, mashed or smashed, Otto loves them all. So it was quite fortuitous that Axel and Rosie were planning their next trip to the South American country of Peru. Specifically, to visit the famous Incan ruins of Peru and the most celebrated of all, Machu Picchu. At Machu Picchu, we will also learn about the Peruvians' devotion to the potato.

Ever since high school, Axel had dreamt of visiting the World Heritage Site of Machu Picchu. His Spanish teacher, Mr. Falanga, would often tell exotic stories about this remote Incan settlement thought to have been constructed in about the year 1450 and located high up in the Andes Mountains of Peru. Mr. Falanga spoke with such embellishment and enthusiasm that Axel had developed a vivid image of what this summer retreat of Inca royals could look like and hoped to make the long journey to the South American continent one day. And that day had finally arrived.

At this point, Axel and Rosie were such skilled travelers that undertaking a lengthy airplane trip didn't really phase them much. But the flight to Miami from DC is about 2 ½ hours and the subsequent trip to Lima, the capital of Peru, takes another 5 hours and 47-ish minutes. That doesn't include a layover time of about 1 hour and 37 minutes. Would Otto and Gidget be able to stay in their transportation housing units for so long? Axel and Rosie certainly hoped so.

Traveling from North to South America is actually a bit easier than flying to Europe. Axel and Rosie's previous flights from DC to Switzerland and Italy had been a maximum of

7 hours and 57 minutes. In this instance, total flight time to Lima, Peru is very similar but there is only a one-hour time difference to Lima compared to DC, not six hours as it is to mainland Europe. You definitely don't feel as discombobulated when you arrive.

Even more interesting, however, is that Peru lies south of the equator, not north like DC or the European countries, and for that reason the seasons are reversed: Axel and Rosie left DC on a cold day in December with seven inches of snow on the ground and when they arrived in Lima it was summertime. Yes, and warm: 77 degrees and balmy. Otto and Gidget would surely be pleased since they hadn't been able to hang out in Rosie and Axel's rear courtyard for several weeks since it had been brrrrrrrrrrr cold.

Another weird phenomenon in traveling to Peru from the east coast of the United States is that you fly nearly due south along the Atlantic coastline but when you arrive in Lima you end up along the Pacific coast. What's up with that? Well, have a look at a globe of the world and you'll see this is just how the North and South American continents are situated to one another.

First things first. Rosie and Axel had booked an organized trip for their stay in Peru since they were unfamiliar with the country and didn't speak a lot of Spanish. It was also much easier as all tours, hotels and meals were organized by the travel group. And this group was particularly special: cats under seventeen pounds were allowed.

The trip turned out to be a breeze: Otto and Gidget were super relaxed and hadn't even realized the airplane had landed. The group was picked up at the airport by a hotel shuttle for the drive into downtown Lima. A limit of seven couples with one cat per couple had been allowed. Everyone was now packed into the vehicle which, in addition to humans, now carried six cats and one ferret. (The ferret's owner had been given special dispensation since just days before the journey she had lost her twentyseven-year-old Manx cat.) The group would only be spending two days sightseeing in Lima since the focus of the trip was on visiting Incan ruins in and around Cuzco, Peru.

I get pretty worked up when describing this adventure and there is so much to know before we begin. Please don't despair as I attempt to set the scene…It might be a little like an Indiana Jones movie, if you happen to be familiar with those. Amazing adventures.

The Incas were a very powerful tribe of South American Indians and ruled an empire extending along the Pacific coast from Northern Ecuador to central Chile during the early 1400's A.D. to the 1530's. That is when they were conquered by Spanish conquistadors, explorers sent out to colonize new nations for purposes of trade. Inca leaders resisted the Spaniards for quite some time but were finally defeated when their last city (Vilcabamba, Peru) was captured in 1572. Say it out loud: Vill-ka-bomb-ba. Love that.

After two days of intense sightseeing in Lima, the highlight being a tour of the pre-Incan ruins of Huaca Pucllana (crazily located in a very dense urban neighborhood), the group took a quick flight high up into the Andes mountains to the city of Cuzco. Almost immediately after arriving at the airport the group boarded their bus and …left town. You may wonder why the tour departed Cuzco so soon but there are a few things you need to know.

Cuzco is situated 3,400 meters above sea level (about 11,157-ish feet) and this causes many people to suffer from altitude sickness. The effects of altitude sickness can be quite unpleasant and may lead to headaches, nausea, nose bleed, dizziness and problems sleeping. (If you're really into the science of what is happening, this icky feeling is due to what is called barometric or atmospheric pressure. This is the pressure of the air that surrounds us all the time. At higher elevations, like Cuzco, this pressure drops and there is less oxygen available to breathe. It takes your body time to adjust since most people don't normally live up in the clouds.)

So this particular trip was designed to help people acclimate slowly to these heights by first visiting Incan ruins at lower elevations and then culminating with those in Cuzco, capital of the Inca Empire AND another UNESCO World Heritage Site. Are you having déjà vu? (I'm just trying to impress you with my vast knowledge of French.)

Okay, back to our tour and, hopefully at some point, potatoes. As Otto and Gidget snoozed on the bus from Cuzco airport, the group visited well-known Incan ruins in Pisaq and Ollantaytambo where the technical talents of these progressive people were on display. The Incas constructed complex watering systems to irrigate their crops which were often located on dizzyingly steep agricultural terraces. They also had an uncanny and mysterious ability to move massive boulders. I mean HUGE: somehow they transported stone blocks weighing more than 100 metric tons (220,462.262185 pounds...that's a lot of decimal places) and often having dimensions as large as 4.5 x 3.2 x 1.7 meters (14.8 x 10.5 x 5.6 feet). They hauled these behemoths through rivers, up mountain faces and to heights of over 2400 meters (7875 feet). Stonemasons would then position the boulders together with such astonishing precision that no mortar was necessary. But the group was particularly pumped up (get it?, water?, irrigation?) for tomorrow's visit to the most majestic of all Incan ruins, the cloud-shrouded city, high up in the Andes Mountains: Machu Picchu.

We've kind of lost track of our travelers but the aura of Incan civilization is so magical that I didn't want to neglect giving you a bit of background. The unique allure of Machu Picchu, however, is probably due to the fact that it lay hidden, covered by vegetation for almost 400 years. That was until the American explorer, Hiram Bingham, rediscovered it in 1911 after years of searching the jungles of Peru. Machu Picchu's existence had been conjectured in many ancient documents but it was only due to Bingham's perseverance that this treasure was brought to light again.

Try to imagine the sensation and thrill Hiram Bingham must have felt when he entered Machu Picchu through its Sun Gate for the first time. Below him lay the ruins he had so persistently sought, the mysterious "citadel in the clouds", abandoned centuries earlier by the Incas. You too will get goosebumps. And on this steep slope stood Axel, Rosie, Otto, and Gidget, together with their fellow explorers, just before sunrise on December 21. As the sun slowly appeared over the mountain ridges to the east, it began to illuminate the remains of foundations of homes, markets, sacrificial altars, bridges and, the most significant structure of all, the Torreon; a dramatic, panoramic view of the lost city of Machu Picchu. The group descended the cobblestone path into the heart of the city, passing walls, battlements and towers which had enabled the Incas to defend their settlement from potential invaders. After several hours of walking and absorbing the architectural feats, they had all built up a serious appetite. And so it begins…

Special preparations had been made to demonstrate how the Incas might have celebrated one of their most significant religious holidays. But first let's assume today is "Opposite Day" for those of us who usually live in the Northern Hemisphere. (I have re-written the following explanation so many times because it never ceases to confuse me with each reread of the text.) Here goes: in the next paragraph, winter is summer and summer is winter....

With our previous discussion of the Sun Gate, you might not be surprised to learn that the Incas worshiped the sun, the most powerful star in our galaxy. Because of this, the Winter Solstice on June 21 and the Summer Solstice on December 21, i.e. the shortest and longest days of the year in Peru, were of great significance. "Ay caramba"! Oh, my goodness. Axel and Rosie had purposefully planned to be at Machu Picchu on the very day the Incas bid farewell to the sun, December 21. They were known to give lavish offerings to Sapa Inca, their Sun God. Axel had intentionally chosen this day rather than June 21 since this latter celebration is truly mayhem: thousands of people congregate at Machu Picchu to party. But today would also be a serious time to boogy.

Pandemonium abounded in the high mountain air as unfamiliar aromas wafted all about. Bountiful offerings were being brought out to honor Sapa Inca as joyful singing took place. The tour group's guide, Freddy, explained how locals would play the roles of Inca nobles by dressing in bejeweled cloaks and robes for a ritual reenactment of this special day. A formal ceremony, about to happen, would include multiple potato-based offerings to Sapa Inca and be unlike anything they had ever tasted.

I bet you assumed I'd never get back to talking spuds. (Obviously, I went off the deep end in my enthusiasm for describing Machu Picchu.) What you need to know is that Peru is home to about 4000 varieties of native potatoes. That's not a typo. Potatoes come in all shapes, sizes and colors: red, blue, pink, yellow, and purple. Peruvians value the humble potato so much that they celebrate each year on National Potato Day, May 30th. Regardless of whether one dines in a rustic village establishment or in a fancy restaurant, potatoes are a mainstay of the cuisine and a staple of Peruvians' diets at home. You will appreciate this info as the culinary aspect of our Summer Solstice festival commences. Magical things are about to happen. But where?

It was logical that the group was now seated within the Torreón, the most impressive structure at Machu Picchu. Within its semi-circular design, Incan architects positioned two windows so precisely that valuable decisions critical to the peoples' livelihood could be made. Through one window, the angle of the light at sunrise on the day of the Summer Solstice (NOW), accurately illuminated a carved altar stone at the base of the Torreon. Spooky. With this knowledge, plans could be made for the ideal time to plant crops or to determine the success of future harvests. Through the other window, the positions of specific constellations and stars were also used to make similar predictions. The Incas were so grateful for the accuracy of these readings that they celebrated their prosperity with annual festivals and generous offerings to the deities. And that is why so many people turn out to commemorate these special days in Incan history, our diverse group of sojourners, cats and ferret included. You could cut the air with a potato masher… Many Incan relics found over the ages also included depictions of jaguars. To which animal family does the jaguar belong? Some scientists even posit that the jaguar was so significant to the Incas they were thought to connect people to the spirit world. Hold on to this thought as the festival begins…

Everything was in place. Priority had been given to Rosie

and Axel's group and they had front row seats as the chanting began and potato dishes were brought forth. If cats could drool, wait, maybe they can, the scents emanating from the extravagantly decorated table in front of the Torreon's "usnu", or altar stone, were enough to make a **cat**erpillar drool: Papa a lattuancaina - boiled potatoes in a spicy cheese sauce and Causa Rellena - layers of mashed potatoes with mixed veggies and fish. Before the feast began, praise was given to a large replica of Sapa Inca, son of the Sun (a homophone, perhaps?). The sculpture had been placed atop the usnu together with an imposing drawing of a jaguar mid-leap.

The ceremony began:

> Praise be Intip Churin (Son of the Sun), graced by the sacred Mascapaicha (Imperial Crown) and bearing the holy Topayauri (Scepter) in Your powerful grip.
> Oh divine One, Sapa Apu, Inka Qhapaq (Mighty Inca), Huaccha Khoyaq (Lover and Benefactor of the Poor).
> We praise You with overwhelming gratitude for Your protective powers!
> ETC. ETC. ETC.
>
> And then abruptly ended with:
> "Ama sua, ama llula, ama cheklla"
> ("Do not steal, do not lie, do not be lazy")

With these final words, our visitors had indeed come closer to understanding this renowned tribe whose scruples and values are, to a certain extent, worthy of emulation.

Humans and the up-until-now-sort-of-patient kitties lapped

up the potato delicacies, not a thought given to the significance of the sun or jaguars. Otto was definitely in heaven. Even Gidget, not a big fan of potatoes, seemed to be inhaling her food, not much chewing going on, and Rosie had to intervene occasionally so she could take a breath of air.

The feast continued until about 2:27 pm at which point Freddy, the tour guide, suggested the cats be allowed to imbibe in a traditional corn cider beverage to wash down all the starchy potatoes. Otto and Gidget took a few nips of the brew but were not convinced of its merit and soon returned to licking their plates in hope of finding any last remnants....

Visiting Machu Picchu was a totally mesmerizing adventure but the meal and rituals our group was able to partake in were truly transcendent. You know what that means? When creating your list for trips of a lifetime, with pets (or without?), put Machu Picchu at the top.

Cheesy Potatoes

6 medium potatoes
½ cup butter
¼ cup grated cheese
1 teaspoon garlic powder
1 teaspoon paprika powder
Salt and pepper, to taste

Slice potatoes very thin; a food processor is great for this. Place them in a large mixing bowl. Melt butter in the microwave and pour over the sliced potatoes. Mix well. Add remaining ingredients and mix. Place everything in a ceramic baking dish big enough for the potatoes to be at a height of about 1 ½ inches. Bake for 35 minutes at 375 degrees. The potatoes should be golden brown and a bit crispy on top.

CHAPTER 5

Otto Sups at the Salmon Buffet (Hegeberg, Sweden)

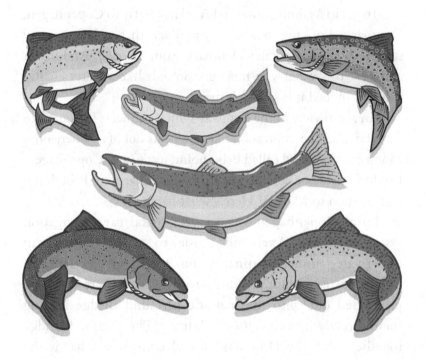

ROSIE AND AXEL were on their way to Malmö, Sweden to attend the wedding of Axel's first cousin, Orlando. Orlando was marrying a wonderful Swedish lady, Petra, who had grown up outside this charming city located in the southern portion of the country. Rosie and Axel were very excited about another adventure with Otto and Gidget and had taken 7 days off from work in order to make the trip. Following the wedding, they planned to vacation along the coast of southwestern Sweden.

To get to Malmö, Rosie and Axel had to fly to Copenhagen, Denmark. Looking at a map you'll see that only a narrow stretch of water separates Denmark from Sweden. And under and over this water you must go. Sounds like a water coaster ride but indeed it is so much more.

An aerial view of the highway which connects Denmark to Sweden gives the impression that it appears out of nowhere onto a long narrow island called Peberholm, just east of Copenhagen. But how does one actually get from Copenhagen to Peberholm and then on to Malmö? Here's what happens:

From Copenhagen airport, the rental car's navigation system directed Axel and Rosie to travel through an underwater tunnel terminating on Peberholm, an artificial island constructed for just this purpose. From there the route proceeded out onto the majestic Oresund Bridge leading them directly into the city of Malmö. (The Oresund Bridge together with the Drogden Tunnel constitute what is the longest combined road and rail bridge in Europe: about 9.87 miles. What a construction project that must have been.) The passenger train is on a dedicated level running just below the highway. Axel found this particularly exciting since one of his great passions as a boy, together with his brother Philip, had been model trains. Philip, especially, would yell from the back seat of the family car whenever he spotted a train: "ZaZa!" And now, Axel was in the driver's seat steering the car over the massive Oresund Bridge on his way to Sweden. Also pretty exciting.

Otto and Gidget began to stir in the back seat just as they arrived in Malmö. They were entirely unaware, of course, that they had traveled from one country to the next in just under 17 minutes. Out the car windows everyone could see attractive cobblestone squares surrounded by half-timbered houses and presently they pulled up to their hotel, The Plaza, selected because they welcomed.....pets.

Cousin Orlando had proposed that Otto and Gidget serve as ring bearers for the wedding and Axel thought the idea could be fun for the gregarious cats. The ceremony was to be held at a small country church followed by a reception at an old, unassuming manor house about 7 miles outside of Malmö.

On the day of the wedding, Otto and Gidget knew something was up when Rosie pulled two embroidered silky vests from the suitcase, one in light blue and the other in pink. Gidget wanted nothing to do with this silly fashion statement and wriggled and squirmed as Rosie tried to button it up. She firmly verbalized her disapproval, screeching at a pitch their fellow hotel guests must have found quite annoying. Otto, on the other hand, was not perturbed at all as Axel buttoned up the vest and held him up to a mirror. Eventually, Gidget realized she wasn't going to rid herself of the satiny apparel and was quickly distracted by a **cat**nip-filled cuddly toy. The foursome left to attend the wedding with everyone looking like the cat's pajamas.

The wedding ceremony was way too long and Axel and Rosie were relieved when Otto and Gidget had fulfilled their duty of delivering the rings to the happy couple. The cats had teetered down the chapel's main aisle with Petra's ring velcroed to Gidget's pink vest and Orlando's attached to Otto's. The reception following the wedding was a blast especially since the cats could romp around the field surrounding the manor house; it was completely fenced in. There was lots of dancing and merry making and a wonderful spread of Swedish delicacies. But they were all saving their appetites for the highlight of the trip and of our story: a fishy feast at the Laxbutik.

The next day Rosie and Axel left Malmö and hit the road heading north to the town of Ugglarp. The town is located along the Skagerrak, the waterway connecting the North Sea to the Baltic Sea, and known for its wild currents which have sunk many a ship. The couple had rented the same vacation house Axel's family had when he was about seven years old. He remembered that trip fondly, taken together with his father's brother, wife and their children. The house lay at the end of a dirt road in a rocky cove along the North Sea. At that time, Axel had spent hours with Uncle Gerd hanging out on the worn wooden steps which ended directly in the water. The main activity was snagging mussels which clung stealthily to the rocks along the shoreline. Axel's job was to gently pry a mussel from one of the rocks, open the shell just a bit, and hand it to Uncle Gerd who would then thread a string through the small slit which was now exposed. The mussels were used as tasty bait to lure scurrying crabs from the shallow waters of the sea. Once caught, the crabs were placed in a bucket so they could be observed up close. Catch and release was the name of the game and after detailed study was complete, they were freed back into the water. Axel and Uncle Gerd were so caught up in this fascinating activity that the rest of the gang often had to bang on a pot to let them know dinner was served.

The vacation house in Ugglarp was just as bizarre as Axel remembered and he hoped that favorable weather would allow them to be outside ALL of the time: Many vacation homes in Sweden serve as full time residences for their owners who often choose to rent them out in the summer to tourists in order to supplement their income. And so, houses are often furnished with all of the owners' possessions and in this case, way too many possessions.... stifling many possessions.....do you get my drift? In every room of Axel and Rosie's rental house there were shelves laden with collections of baskets, (creepy) dolls, clocks, cutting boards, photographs, fishing memorabilia, medical devices you don't want to know about...The small and only bathroom in the house was equipped with bars to hang towels, bars to hold onto, bars to support bars....And so, the goal was to be outside whenever possible so as not to succumb to claustrophobia. To do that, every transportable table was carried out to the flagstone patio so one could sit for hours and avoid being inside. Except to sleep, of course. But the location... You couldn't ask for more when every evening promised a spectacular sunset on the patio, refreshing breezes off the sea, and the day's activities up for discussion.

But first things first. Shortly after arriving and unloading the car, Axel ran down to the cove, Gidget in tow (naturally in her transportation housing), to see if any mussels or crabs could be spotted in the sea. And yes. He placed Gidget's carrying case on the ground and hopped down the steps, even more worn out than he recollected, and peered into the crystal clear water. Mussels galore. And the pint-sized crabs from his times with Uncle Gerd were there too. Gidget would have been well served (!) if Axel could only have let her out of the case. But he knew that tomorrow she would be more than satisfied with their outing to the Laxbutik.

As I describe the Laxbutik, or literally "The Salmon Shop", your mouth will certainly begin to water. Truly. And a lot. Especially if you love salmon which, of course, Rosie and Axel did and, how could you think Otto and Gidget wouldn't. The no-frills, nondescript, one-story building set within a rather unattractive parking lot was just off the ramp of the Hegeberg highway exit. And it might be easy to miss but if you do, I can only say "sa sorgligt", how sad. Just 27 minutes from the vacation house in Ugglarp, an exquisite experience awaits those not deterred by the simple building and the corny, azure-colored neon sign blinking quietly atop the glassed-in entrance. But step inside....

Pets allowed, of course, and the foursome entered into salmon heaven. Greeted at the door by a dapper-looking older man wearing a salmon-colored apron, the group was escorted to a lovely booth with a view to a portion of the North Sea known as the Kattegat (rhymes with kitty cat?). The fantastically, fabulous, fish buffet stretched around three sides of the main dining room and was brimming with every salmon creation imaginable. In case you've never experienced a buffet, it is a self-serve, choose what you like, as much as you like, and come back as many times as you like, food extravaganza. In other words, ...cataclysmically crazy.

The food was covered by clear glass canopies to protect it from sneezers and coughers, and the selection was overwhelming:

salmon bisque (that's soup), blackened salmon, cured salmon, salmon tartare (that's raw fish), grilled and smoked and pickled salmon, fresh and tasty salmon salad, salmon sushi and taco rolls, pepper-crusted salmon, salmon quiche with spinach, salmon croquettes and for dessert, cheesecake topped with salmon roe (those are eggs….).

As you can imagine, once Axel and Rosie's plates from the buffet were filled, with a plethora of fish selections for Otto and Gidget of course, everyone settled into or onto the table (that was allowed here) and there reigned a state of utter silence. There was too much fishy goodness to be savored for idle chit chat. After about 7 trips up to the buffet, Otto and Gidget collapsed onto Axel and Rosie's laps. They were again in a similar state to that of their first overseas trip to Verbier: simply **cat**atonic.

Time in Hegeberg flew by with many yummy meals on the patio facing the sea. One in particular was almost worthy of comparison with dinner at the Laksbutik but still….. not really. What could be any better? In a distant second place was their meal on the evening before they were set to return to the United States. Rosie had prepared it as a surprise based on what Axel had described as another culinary extravaganza he and his family had had years ago.

The long dining table on the patio was spread with brown packing paper (what do you think that's all about?) on which the usual dinner plates and glassware had been set. But there were a few unusual additions: blue and yellow bibs, the cheerful colors of the Swedish national flag, had been placed at everyone's dinner plate together with what looked like a stainless steel nutcracker. But this utensil would not be used to crack nuts.

Axel donned his bib and waited patiently at the table for the arrival of the secret meal. And out came Rosie carrying a ginormous platter piled high with langoustines. You are of course wondering what these might be, so here goes. There is some debate whether to call these seafood creatures big shrimp or mini lobsters. So the choice is up to you. Regardless, these rare "shrim-sters" (I couldn't decide) are one of the most exquisite tasting seafoods on the entire planet. With a divine texture and sublime flavor, these slender delicacies contain the sweetest meat in their tails and claws. And to reach those tight places, the cracking tools would be implemented. The lobsterettes/ gargantuan shrimps (what's with this indecision..) produced such a wonderful waft that Otto and Gidget were soon jolted out of their late afternoon nap. Up they sprung from the window seat facing the patio and begged to be let out for dinner.

As mentioned before, eating outdoors was the preferred option at the house in Ugglarp. Axel and Rosie were initially stumped as to how they might accommodate the cats on the patio without the necessity to confine them in their housing units. A clever idea was hatched by transforming a mesh, baby playpen found in the attic (there was EVERYTHING in this house…) into an outdoor space for Otto and Gidget by simply flipping it over.

And here they all were, everyone sporting a colorful bib, and about to enjoy the freshest North Sea treat imaginable. The langoustines were incredible and Gidget, but especially Otto, was crazy about the new taste experience. They sat for hours, isolating bits of meat which were dunked into small cups of melted butter, popped into their mouths, and savored. A slow, languid meal on their last night in Sweden.

Clean up was a breeze since all uneaten parts of the langoustines had been placed directly onto the packing paper with which the table had been covered. Roll it up and toss. Axel was thrilled with the unexpected meal and he and Rosie were already discussing the possibility of a family reunion next year in Ugglarp.

Maple Salmon*

¼ cup maple syrup.
2 tablespoons soy sauce
1 clove garlic, minced
¼ teaspoon garlic powder
⅛ teaspoon ground black pepper
1 pound salmon

Mix all ingredients together except salmon in a bowl. Place salmon in a shallow baking dish and pour maple syrup mixture over the top. Flip the salmon a few times until it is coated all over. Marinate in the fridge for 30 minutes, turning once. Remove fish from the fridge and let stand as you preheat the oven to 400 degrees. Bake fish, uncovered for 20 minutes, or until it flakes easily with a fork.

*allrecipes.com

CHAPTER 6

Otto Rises to the Challenge: Raclette in the Rockies AND Never Use "Beef" as a Password (Vail, Colorado)

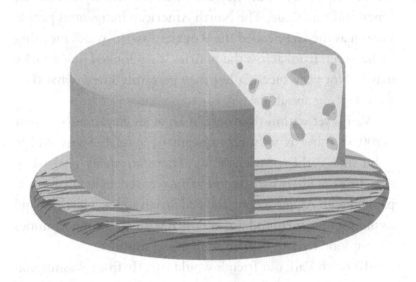

OTTO AND GIDGET were packing up or, more precisely, being packed up for their annual ski retreat into the Rocky Mountains. At this point they were very "seasoned" (it's all about food, isn't it?) travelers and didn't need much encouragement to slip into their transportation housing. However, Rosie continued to prepare their carry-on cases with a little splash of **cat**nip and the cats' favorite blankets but honestly it probably wasn't even necessary since they were always up for a new adventure.

The family was heading to Vail, Colorado, a quaint little town in the heart of the Rocky Mountains, more commonly known as the "Rockies". You might wonder why the Rockies are called "rocky" but they are just that. Mostly sandstone, limestone, and shale. The North American indigenous people known as the Cree called the Rockies "as-sin-wati" meaning "when seen from across the prairies, they looked like a rocky mass". Not very succinct but they certainly knew what they were talking about.

Vail is set within this rocky mass at an elevation of almost 8,200 feet and is very reminiscent of a small Swiss village (a bit like Verbier, Switzerland). There are many chalet-like structures with ornate wood trim, carved balconies, walls painted with Alpine scenes, and pedestrian zones. The town and its picturesque surroundings are filled with many opportunities for outdoor activity both in winter and summer.

To reach Vail, our friends would first fly from Washington DC to Denver, the capital of Colorado. The flight itself progressed rather well except for a few, namely two, rather loud disturbances. Rosie and Axel had pacified Otto and Gidget as usual and the cats had already been pretty laid back on the way to the airport. However, a few minutes into the flight a series of sharp, piercingly loud **cat**calls caused many passengers to hop up to determine where the ruckus was coming from. Even Axel was concerned that Otto might be coming out of his coma-like state since he was known to yowl quite passionately when looking for attention. Axel leaned forward to check under the seat, unzipped the top of the mesh case and eased out Otto's head to see if all was copacetic. Nada. Otto gazed back with big-pupiled, glazed over eyes, as if to say, "wasn't me". Axel also saw that Gidget was still completely zonked out. Satisfied they were not at fault, the question became who's cats were. The high-pitched howls continued intermittently until the end of the 3 hour 7 minute flight after which the mystery was solved. **Cat**ty-corner to where Rosie and Axel had been sitting, a young man rose to exit the plane. Not only did he have one cat in the required traveling case but two…He nonchalantly ducked out without a word of contrition to any of the other passengers who had endured one of the noisiest flights EVER.

Now settled into their rental car, Rosie steered the group out of the Denver airport for the two hour and 7 minute drive (weather permitting) to Vail. The first portion of the trip is generally pretty tame as one travels through the most western portion of the Great Plains and then into the foothills of the Rockies. The vista is quite dramatic as, from the flatness of the plains, the Rocky Mountains appear to burst out of nowhere. And their snow-covered peaks are a stark contrast to the often barren environs of Denver.

Once arriving at "The Chalet" in Vail (lovingly called so by Axel's parents and, if you remember, what the Swiss usually call their mountain homes), Otto and Gidget set out to explore any changes which might have been made since their last visit. Up and down the two flights of stairs they went, checking out each room, making sure things were as they should be. But a few minutes later they were sprawled out in front of the hearth waiting for Axel to get a fire started.

Hannah and Peter, Axel's parents, were also visiting for the week between Christmas and New Years as was his brother, Philip. Otto was feeling particularly affectionate towards them all since they hadn't been together in Vail for about a year. Hannah, who was a children's book author, couldn't get much writing done since every time she was at her desk Otto draped himself over her shoulders and purred like a locomotive. In all honesty, it was difficult for Hannah to disengage from Otto since she herself was feeling a bit affection-deprived. Otto would rub cheeks with her, positioning himself for maximum facial contact. His front paws dangled over Hannah's right shoulder and his tail swayed quietly back and forth over the left.

Otto was especially lovey-dovey as Christmas Eve approached. A winter storm was forecast and I'm guessing he was feeling somewhat perturbed as windows rattled and gusts of wind came down the flue and shook the exhaust flap in the kitchen. Hannah could see the approaching snowfall coming in from the west as Otto tightened his grip around her neck. Snow soon began falling at a rate of several inches an hour. What purrfect timing for a raclette dinner with the whole family together again in the mountains. A big meow to that.

Hannah had set up the raclette machine on the dining table, a device which improvises on the traditional meal served in many Alpine restaurants. Instead of an electric heat source under which a big wheel of raclette sits and from which portions of hot gooey cheese are scraped off with a wire, this home version allows everyone to be in control of their own portions of cheese. A piece of raclette cheese, about 7 by 7 centimeters, is placed in a small pan and slid under the electric coil of the machine, right next to the neighbor's pan. Very cozy in oh so many ways.

(Before I describe the other main ingredient of the meal, melted raclette cheese is also traditionally served with tiny French pickles called "cornichons". Many people might prefer other jarred sour veggies like onions, cauliflower or whole baby corn spears. You'll see that Otto could have cared less about any of these when you learn what else was on the menu.)

Of course, the aromatic scent of cheese being sliced in preparation for the meal caused Otto to **cat**apult into the kitchen. Lurking around the kitchen island, he lost all sense of decorum and stretched his entire body up to counter height hoping to obtain a pre-meal sample. Axel's dad, Peter, was a real pushover for Otto and slipped him a few tidbits before anyone could see.

And now, here it comes: the other component of a traditional raclette meal is boiled and peeled potatoes. (You recall Otto's adventure at Machu Picchu and how much he adored potatoes. I would now say they were his second favorite food after cheese.) So here we go: Everyone is assembled at the table waiting for their pan of cheese to bubble and melt. That first slice always seems to take an eternity…. During this process the cooked potatoes are passed around for peeling. A small paring knife tests the agility of diners to remove the skin from a hot potato. This alone adds to the fun and ambiance. Ouch. But most lovely of all is that raclette is an absolutely leisurely and social meal: cheese slowly melts, potatoes are peeled (more or less slowly) and time flies by. The room becomes warm and cozy from the heat emanating from the raclette machine and any stress of the day is soon forgotten.

Otto waited (sort of) politely for Rosie to prepare his very own dish. (I forgot to tell you that Gidget had had a very stressful day napping and was continuing to nap downstairs under the covers of Rosie and Axel's bed.) Rosie chopped up a bit of potato into bite-sized pieces, took a pan out of the raclette machine, and poured the melted cheese over the top. As a final touch, she ground some fresh pepper on top and placed it in front of Otto. You might have a sneaking suspicion of his reaction when presented with two of his favorite foods. Intense, enthusiastic purring nearly masked the din of conversation.

After 7 servings of raclette Otto was finally sated and, with the warmest, happiest feeling in his tummy, silently retreated to join his sister under the down blanket on the bed. In the meantime, Axel's brother Philip challenged everyone to beat his all-time record of 17 servings of cheese. And so dinner continued.....

Snowfall persisted throughout the next week allowing for some glorious "powder" skiing on the slopes. It was New Year's Eve and the family lined up at the big windows in the living room preparing for a celebratory fireworks display. With an unobstructed view down the Vail valley they were able to enjoy a colorful presentation taking place at the base of the ski mountain. And what a show it was. Even though they were about 2.7 miles from where the fireworks were being shot up, they could still hear the boom and bang they made. This was way too much commotion for Gidget and Otto and they quickly scampered to the downstairs bathroom which had no windows and so significantly dampened the noise from outside.

Everyone was feeling quite invigorated following the

dazzling show and had built up a healthy appetite for which Peter and Hannah had prepared...

Axel had grown up eating Beef Stroganoff, a favorite dish which Hannah prepared on special occasions. You might wonder what "Stroganoff" means and I'll be as brief as possible so we can get down to the eating. There is an old city in western Russia called Veliky Novgorod, also a World Heritage Site (... they're everywhere). Anyway, in the 18th century a prominent Russian merchant family by the name of Stroganoff lived there.

I can't tell you exactly why the classic dish of "Beef Stroganoff" is named after this family, and you might want to put that into research, but they were so influential to the Russian economy, particularly in the region of Siberia, that they were inducted into the aristocracy. That's a big deal. And so is the meal the family was about to partake in, particularly for Otto. Yet again.

This finally brings us to part of the title of this chapter: "... Never Use Beef as a Password"...But why? Because it isn't Stroganoff.....Strong enough? Ugh. Excuse my punny sense of humor but sometimes I just can't help myself when trying to describe this mouthwatering dish.

To create Beef Stroganoff, strips of tenderloin are quickly sautéed (pan fried at high temperature) in butter and then combined with onions, mushrooms and sour cream. A dash of Dijon mustard, (check out where that originates from...très bien), and salt and pepper are added to the sauce and voilà.. That means we're ready to get the meal started.

Would you like to guess what Hannah chose to serve the Stroganoff with? Not rice, not pasta (although that tastes pretty good, too), but boiled potatoes. Simple to make and Otto's second favorite food.

Since this would be their last family dinner together in

Vail before Rosie and Axel left the next morning to return to Washington, DC, they were feeling somewhat generous towards Otto and Gidget knowing they would be confined to their travel cases for about 7 hours. Axel descended the steps to rouse the cats for dinner but Otto and Gidget already knew there was more than cat food on the menu. Before Axel had even reached the lower level landing, a blur of fur swooshed by and up the stairs.

The table was set, candles lit, lights turned down low, Gidget's favorite Taylor Swift music murmuring softly in the background, and hunger heightening. The cats were perched on counter-high stools at the middle of the table facilitating an unobstructed view in all directions. Gidget was actually content just hanging out after having already satisfied her appetite with kitty kibble. However, you might have guessed Otto knew exactly that cat food would have been a waste of critical tummy capacity. And you would be correct. This people-food meal required his full commitment.

A layer of potatoes followed by a few spoonfuls of Beef Stroganoff, a side salad of spinach with dried cherries and pear, and the family was ready to say "Priyatnogo appetita"! I bet you can guess what that means. Bon appetit, guten Appetit, or enjoy your meal! Almost like being in Veliky Novgorod? Not quite, but everyone was still grateful to indulge in this unique culinary creation in the coziness of The Chalet.

Until we "meat" again!

Beef Stroganoff

100 grams butter or canola oil
300 grams onions, thinly sliced
250 grams fresh mushrooms, thinly sliced
Salt
Ground pepper
1 tablespoon mustard
750 grams beef tenderloin, cut into thin strips approx. 2" x ¼"
¼ liter sour cream

Using a metric scale to weigh ingredients is a great way to get a feeling for a different form of measurement. If you don't have access to one, find a conversion chart to convert the amounts given into ounces.

Melt half the butter in a large skillet over medium high heat. Sauté the thinly sliced onions and mushrooms (again, a food processor is great for this) for about 5 minutes, stirring occasionally. Mix in salt, pepper and mustard and cook a few minutes longer. Place the mixture in a bowl. In the same skillet, melt the remaining butter, turn up the heat to high and sauté the beef strips. Stir continuously. Once the meat has lost its red color, turn down the heat, add the veggies back into the pan, mix to combine, stir in sour cream and simmer gently until warm. Correct spices to taste.

CHAPTER 7

Otto Falls For a Fellow Feline (Nikko, Japan)

WE ARE ABOUT to embark on our final adventure with Otto and Gidget, loved ones in tow. The trip takes us on our longest journey thus far and to another remarkable World Heritage Site rife with shrines and temples: Nikko, Japan.

Let's set the scene for the fun to come: Axel's most memorable family vacation had been the Spring Break trip of his senior year in high school. He, Hannah and Peter met up in Japan with Philip, a junior in college at the time, for what would become their last trip together as a family of four. And so, in itself, this was a very special experience and, the fact that it was such an exotic journey, made it even more extraordinary. After sightseeing in Tokyo and Kyoto (we'll perhaps need to visit these spectacular places in our next book of excursions and victuals, oops, I mean food of course), they traveled to the spiritual enclave of Nikko, a few hours train ride north of Tokyo. Nikko ended up being the most awesome part of that trip and Axel always hoped to return with Rosie and the cats and to introduce them to Japan's most famous (sleeping) cat.

 Before I tell you about Axel and Rosie in Nikko, there is a very appropriate tidbit of information I'd like to share: the Japanese adore cats. Maneki-neko are waving feline figures seen in many commercial locales throughout the country, often in front windows of shops, restaurants, and hotels. These cats are not waving hello or goodbye but beckoning you to come closer.

Let me now impress upon you just how far Japan is from the east coast of the United States: Flights from Washington DC to Osaka, the airport into which Rosie and Axel would fly, are 17 hours long (☺), including one stop. In addition to that crazy thought, you also need to know that DC time is 13 hours behind Japan. So try to imagine, it is Thursday, July 7 at 2:27 P.M. in DC and at the exact same moment it is Friday, July 8 and 3:27 A.M. in Japan. Cat got your tongue? Can you imagine Otto and Gidget in their transportation housing for so long? What would happen when they got really hangry? Would the trip become a huge **cat**astrophe for Axel and Rosie?

Dr. Jean was concerned about providing sleepy-making meds for such a long period of time and so a more creative solution was called for: a cat pawty pack. (Any New Yorkers out there?) Okay, we're getting into some uncharted territory here but I'm hoping the adults in your life will forgive me as I tread into deeper waters. (What I am about to explain is a bit reminiscent of Butterbeer which, as you Harry Potter fans might recall, was consumed at the Leaky Cauldron in Diagon Alley.) You are likely aware that there are beverages for the under 21 crowd and then those for the "grown up" crowd. A great favorite of the latter is wine and if you know just a little about wine, you may have heard of "Burgundy" or "Riesling" wines. However, there are also "wines", non-alcoholic of course, that have been especially formulated for cats and some of these are cleverly called "Purrgundy" and "Meowsling", respectively. Sort of like Butterbeer. These concoctions are infused with **cat**nip keeping felines gloriously content for hours. And so, it was Axel and Rosie's great hope that Otto and Gidget could be pacified for the many hours confined en route to Japan. Pawty on.

The long journey flew (!) by relatively quickly and Otto and Gidget dozed contentedly in their cases following just a few drops of kitty "wine". Their legs became a bit like jello and they were most content lying on their backs, paws akilter and eyes shut. It was only during the train ride to Nikko that they returned to the world of the awake.

The shrines and temples in Nikko National Park are situated on verdant hillsides surrounded by dense cedar forests. At the base of the Park is the city of Nikko itself which boasts lush emerald mountains and many waterfalls. But Nikko is also home to many hot springs known as "onsen". And here comes a brief word on what those might be:

Japan's over 6000 (!) islands are located on a volcanic fault line in the northwestern Pacific Ocean. Because of this, the earth beneath is very active and water from heated springs emanates from the depths of the ocean at temperatures above 77 degrees Fahrenheit. The Japanese enjoy bathing in these warm waters since they are imbued with minerals and thought to have a multitude of health benefits. One can access hot springs from within many traditional inns called "Ryokans". Not only popular for the chance to relieve bodily ailments and soothe tired joints, Ryokans also offer traditional Japanese cuisine. Another excuse for Otto and company to undertake this lengthy journey? You are correct. Axel, Rosie and the cats planned to spend as much time as possible at The Sehime Monogatari Ryokan between visits to the spiritual sites of Nikko National Park.

The Sehime Monogatari Ryokan which Axel had reserved several months prior to the trip, was in close proximity to the Nikko train station. After a short walk, they checked in at the front desk of the inn which was situated in a tall glass atrium facing lush green slopes. The group was soon led to their room by a lovely, kimono-clad woman named Megumi who stopped in front of a set of sliding doors and instructed Rosie and Axel to place their shoes on trays and step into a pair of wooden sandals called "geta" before entering (Otto and Gidget were excused in this regard.) As the doors slid open, they could see that the room was very sparsely furnished and had floors constructed of tatami mats made of woven straw. Megumi showed Axel and Rosie the blue and white "yukata" hanging in the closet, explaining that these could be worn anywhere in the Ryokan for the duration of their stay. The yukata were bathrobe-type garments held closed by an "obi", or belt, and wearing them was highly encouraged, even at mealtimes, so guests could chill out to the max. Very comfy. Megumi then bowed quietly and left the room so the guests could enjoy the tea she had prepared and discuss strategy for the next few days in Nikko.

After quenching their thirst, Axel proposed stretching their legs (and paws) following their long journey with a brief visit to Nikko National Park. In this way, they'd be able to get their bearings and scope out the sites they were most interested in seeing. Everyone would also build up a hearty appetite for the eleven-course dinner awaiting them at The Ryokan Sehime Monogatari upon their return.

Rosie and Axel had prepared for the trip knowing the cats would need to endure longer periods of time in their travel cases, in- and outdoors. They had had a custom-made buggy constructed so Otto and Gidget could be pushed around the Park without worrying they might suddenly wander off. It was similar to a baby carriage for twins which they were essentially, brother and sister born within minutes of each other. The buggy was equipped with special clamps to accommodate the transportation housing units. With a few quick moves,

Otto and Gidget could be released and carried into the ancient temples and shrines. The lobster-shaped, **cat**nip-infused chewy toys within would hopefully help them put up with a few hours of sightseeing each day.

In order to visit the Nikko World Heritage Site one must cross the red arched Shinkyo Bridge spanning the Daiya River. There is a crazy legend describing a ten-foot tall God called upon to answer the prayers of a pilgrim wishing to cross the Daiya at a time before the bridge had been built. The God summoned two snakes which he then transformed into the shape of a bridge and before the pilgrim's eyes, Shinkyo Bridge appeared. (I envision this mighty God using both arms to create waves out of the snakes' bodies, sort of like ropes used for exercise purposes called "battling ropes".) The group could definitely sense some weird vibes as they crossed the high arching bridge over the swiftly flowing river. Spooky.

Continuing on, they strolled through large swaths of densely-placed, moss-covered lanterns hovering about waist high. Within the Park, the mood was eerily tranquil as low-lying clouds shrouded hundred-foot cedars. Axel made mental notes of the many sites to see over the next few days. However, jet lag was **cat**ching up to them and, after finding a lovely bench with a magnificent view of Ninno-Ji Temple, a gold-encrusted, ornately-carved structure, they took a break until it was time to return to the Ryokan for dinner. Tomorrow they would visit the interior of Ninno-Ji which houses a large sculpture of Buddha called Bato. This extraordinary, all-knowing being is also a deity of the animal kingdom. How fortuitous our tuckered-out travelers relaxed just here.

Back at the Ryokan, Rosie and Axel changed into their yukata and readied Otto and Gidget for dinner. They had reserved a private dining room so the cats could wander about unimpeded. As they entered, they caught a glimpse of two servers in traditional dress peeking around one of the screens, giggling to one another. They had been informed that Otto and Gidget would also be at dinner and were excited to serve this unusual group of visitors.

Axel and Rosie were directed to sit on beautifully embroidered cushions placed on the floor in front of a long wooden table. Pots of green tea were waiting for them, two cups as well as two saucers, just in case the cats wanted to try the piping-hot, herbal beverage.

As soon as Rosie and Axel had (somewhat awkwardly) lowered themselves to the 17-inch low table, and as Otto and Gidget explored the nearly empty tatami-matted room, the servers proceeded to carry in lovely enameled trays laden with multiple tiny plates. The dishes each contained bite-sized bits of fishy deliciousness or veggies which had been harvested from the Ryokan's own gardens. Otto and Gidget quickly caught a whiff of the goodies and settled onto Axel and Rosie's laps waiting to partake.

Sushi, Sashimi, Buri Daikon, Shioyaki Sakana, Katsuo-no-Tataki, Sanma-no-Nitsuke, Miso-zuke Salmon, Nanban-zuke... Girl oh girl, don't ask me what all that means. I just thought it would be fun to try to pronounce the names of these classic Japanese dishes in a language we so seldom hear spoken. In words we might understand, there were multiple kinds of fish: mackerel, sea bream, salmon, tuna, and eel which had been prepared in rice, on rice, in rolls, and in balls. The fish had been breaded, fried, pickled, dried, or grilled. It was served with even more rice, steamed and fried, pickled vegetables and condiments like fresh wasabi, grated ginger, radish and don't forget soy sauce for dunking. The fact of the matter is there was a lot of FISH and two excited felines waiting to dive in.

And they did. One plate at a time and over a period of hours. Otto was particularly smitten with the dried eel skewers which he gently pawed at before popping them in his mouth, followed by some patient chewing (so unlike Otto who normally swallows everything whole). These delectable niblets (is that even a word?) were small nibbles of chewy, savory, salty, mouthwatering lusciousness. Gidget, on the other hand (I mean paw) was a fan of sardines marinated in "mirin", or sweet rice wine, leading us to what Rosie and Axel were sipping.

We previously spoke about adult beverages vs. non-adult beverages, i.e. those your parents or guardians might drink and those you drink. Axel and Rosie were enjoying the former, specifically "sake", an alcoholic beverage of Japanese origin made from fermented rice. This might not seem like a big deal but sake can have an alcohol content of somewhere between 13-17%. As a result, this non-carbonated, sweet libation can really pack a punch even though it is made from just two simple ingredients: rice and water.

Dinner progressed leisurely, everyone in awe of the unusual treats and taste buds aglow from new and curious flavors. Just before they thought the meal was over, a selection of a most refreshing dessert called "mochi", walnut-sized, colorful tidbits, dusted in powdered sugar, was brought into the dining room. The outside of these dainty morsels was made of chewy rice paste and they were filled with creamy ice cream in the traditional Japanese flavors of pistachio, green tea, mango, black sesame, red bean and plum wine. We know Otto loves cheese and to which food group does this belong? Dairy? And ice cream belongs to….? Check. So, who might have been particularly pleased with the dessert following this extraordinary meal?

On returning to their room after dinner, they found that futons had been laid out on the tatami floor. The futon sets included a mattress and duvet (blanket) and were rolled out for sleeping, a bit like camping but much cozier and comfortable. (Futons disappear easily into a closet in the morning so a room can be used for daytime purposes. This is quite practical in traditional inns such as this but also for many Japanese whose homes are often much smaller than those you might be accustomed to.) Otto and Gidget were quite enamored with the futon set up and snuggled in for a peaceful night's sleep.

The next morning everyone was feeling a bit pokey and still quite sated following the multi-course dinner of the previous evening. Because of this, as well as the fact there was quite a long to-do list, Axel and Rosie decided to skip breakfast (generally, not a good idea..) and head for Nikko National Park straight away. They also planned to have a very light dinner that evening so they could save their appetite for the renowned 7-course Japanese breakfast at the Ryokan the following morning. Enough about food. We need to extricate this group to the Park.

First up was Toshogu Shrine, probably one of the most lavish in all Japan. The site houses the tomb of Tokugawa Ieyasu and is one of the most solemn areas in the Park. Ieyasu was a warlord and controlled the entire country by establishing a shogunate (a military dictatorship) which ruled for more than 250 years. On the cedar-lined path leading up to Ieyasu's final resting place is a very famous wooden sculpture of a sleeping cat which, you recall, Axel was anxious to show Otto and Gidget. "Nemuri-Neko" was very lifelike and reclined amongst the trees, guarding over the sacred site and making quite an impression on our visitors. (In Japanese folklore, cats have protective powers and symbolize good fortune.)

Also within Toshogu Shrine is a sacred stable decorated with very elaborate carvings you may even be familiar with. The stable is adorned with three unique monkeys, VERY famous monkeys: the "hear no evil, see no evil, speak no evil" monkeys representing the basic principles of (Tendai) Buddhism. It's really bananas (get it?) to think that this famous proverb, known throughout the world, originated from three monkeys sitting in a remote Japanese forest.

On their final day in Nikko everyone was looking forward to the 7-course breakfast at the Ryokan. This was definitely not your typical frosted flakes or buttered toast kind of breakfast but rather a more serious lunch- or light-dinner- sort of affair. They were again in the private dining room and quickly took their places on the floor cushions, awaiting another round of Japanese treats. Otto and Gidget vividly remembered what had transpired in this room so not much exploring went on. Instead, they settled onto Rosie and Axel's laps.

The servers brought everything in at once and placed the dishes before the curious culinary connoisseurs. The same women who had helped the other evening were there again, having requested that: if "the cat group" shared another meal at the Ryokan, they would be allowed to serve them.

And so it began. First off, steaming hot miso soup served in beautiful, covered, lacquered bowls. This comforting, fish-based broth with tidbits of tofu, seaweed and scallions awoke everyone's taste buds and the cats lapped it up like crazy. Soup for breakfast you might ask, but so yum. Following that, an assortment of delicacies one would not normally have an appetite for so early in the morning but, yes: salted salmon, grilled mackerel, and sweet rolled omelets accompanied by pickled veggies: cucumber, cabbage, and radish. Rosie really loved those. But the funky fermented soybeans had everyone wondering, why? Such a strange flavor and definitely not for the faint of heart. Lastly, spinach with sesame dressing, a big favorite for Axel and Rosie. Throughout the meal, green tea was served from lovely, decorated enamel pots; the ideal beverage with which to wash everything down.

When they had finished, Axel and Rosie lay flat on their backs atop the tatami mats. They had eaten so much and could barely move. Regardless, there was still one more site to visit at the Park before leaving Nikko, the most sacred temple of all, Rinnoji. So get your acts together people! (BTW, Otto and Gidget were also feeling quite lethargic and so willingly slunk into their housing units to be pushed up the breathtaking hills of Nikko one last time.)

I debated whether to tell you about Rinnoji Temple or not but it is such a wonderful note to end our last trip together on. The Temple is also over 1,250 years old so I just had to. I sound like a broken record (do you even know what a "record" is?). There are several special sculptures hidden within Rinnoji: three towering, gold-lacquered, wooden statues each almost 27 feet tall. One of these, Senju-Kannon, supposedly has a thousand arms. Imagine having to carve all those limbs...Axel now stood before the gargantuan being and began to count but stopped... you just have to have faith. Another statue bore the head of a horse, a bit off putting to Otto but Gidget was in a deep snooze and completely unaware. The group silently took in the magnificence of these treasures and, in that moment, was struck by how fortunate they were to be able to travel the world, enriching their lives with the fascinating history and cuisines of countries around the globe.

Afterwards, they reluctantly returned to pack up their belongings at the Ryokan and head to the train which would take them directly to the airport. Once on board, the gentle rocking of the car led to a most pleasant power nap and happy thoughts of Nikko which, so appropriately, means "sunlight". A most extraordinary adventure. And indeed, with the warmth of the sun streaming through the train windows, dreams were permeated with thoughts of their next culinary adventure together. Will you join them? Here's hoping.

Until then, happy travels to all – Hannah

Miso Soup*

2 cups water, chicken broth or vegetable broth (or Dashi**)
4 ounces silken or firm tofu, drained and cut into small cubes ¼"-
½" in size
1-2 scallions, thinly sliced
2 tablespoons red miso paste (see **Note**)

I would recommend that first time miso soup makers use water or broth as a base rather than Dashi** for which you can, however, find an easy recipe at *the kitchn.com.

Place water or broth in a saucepan and heat on medium-high. In a separate bowl, mix miso paste with ½ cup warm broth and whisk until no lumps remain. Pour dissolved miso back into the broth, reduce heat to medium-low and add tofu. Simmer just until the tofu is warm, 1-2 minutes. Do not boil. Scatter scallions over the soup just before serving. The miso may settle so stir again before eating. **Note:** restaurants usually use red miso paste but the soup can also be made with white or yellow miso. It's just a matter of preference. These days you will probably find miso and tofu in the "international" aisle of a grocery store but an Asian food shop will for sure have what you need.

UPCOMING CULINARY ADVENTURES
WITH OTTO and friends:

- Otto Takes On Tuna Town (Portland Wharf, Maine)
- Otto Pledges Allegiance in Our Nation's Capital (Washington, DC)
- Otto Doesn't Waffle (Bruge, Belgium)
- Otto Knows His Knedliky (Prague, Czech Republic)
- Otto Munches Mussels (Concarneau, France)
- Otto Begs for Bourgognione (Burgundy, France)
- Otto Goes on a Grand Cayman Getaway (British Territory)
- Otto Stalks Peacocks (Cuernavaca, Mexico)
- Otto Goes to the "Source": Milking Cows (Hinang, the German Alps)
- Otto Visits Some Fountain Friends at the Alhambra (Granada, Spain)
- Otto Tackles Tokyo (Japan)

And a reminder from Hannah: National Cat Week has been celebrated in the United States during the first full week of November since 1946. Established by the American Feline Society, this week "highlights the intelligence, personalities, and qualities of **cat**s". Otto and Gidget are all in and hold an annual pawty at which they show photos from all their trips of the previous year.

"A unique approach inspiring teens, and maybe a few grownups, to travel the world in search of tradition and treats, both human and feline. Three meows to Hannah on just the beginning of the adventures of Otto and Gidget!"
Mercatores.com

"Many parents seek to expose their children to other cultures and peoples in a way that is understandable and fun. This bodega **cat** and cohorts make it all possible. And the recipes "cater" to all those culinary creatives who want to take these travels to the next level: right into their own kitchens!"
Global-Outcomes.com

About the Author

H.K. SCRIBNICK began her writing career by promoting the natural sciences to high school students who often see the field as nerdy or intimidating. She then worked in Germany preparing, writing and editing documentation required to conduct clinical trials for the pharmaceutical industry. Later, she became a grant writer for a small non-profit to fund outreach programming for underserved communities. With "The Culinary Adventures of a Brooklyn Bodega Cat", she has finally been able to transition from very structured to very creative writing. The stories recounted here are based on the memorable travels she and her family have had together. H.K. Scribnick graduated from Vassar College with a B.A. in Biopsychology.

Printed in the United States
by Baker & Taylor Publisher Services